TYLER TOAD
AND THE THUNDER

TYLER TOAD
AND THE THUNDER

by Robert L. Crowe

illustrated by Kay Chorao

A PUFFIN UNICORN

Unicorn is a registered trademark of Dutton Children's Books.

Library of Congress number 80-347
ISBN 0-14-054791-6

Published in the United States by Dutton Children's Books.
a division of Penguin Books USA Inc.
375 Hudson Street, New York, N.Y. 10014

Editor: Ann Durell   Designer: Riki Levinson

Printed in Hong Kong by South China Printing Co.
First Unicorn Edition 1986   W
10 9 8 7 6 5

To my wife Sandy—
I have enough wind for the sail
but your love and encouragement
have been the rudder.
R.L.C.

For B. F. Sproat, my mother
K.C.

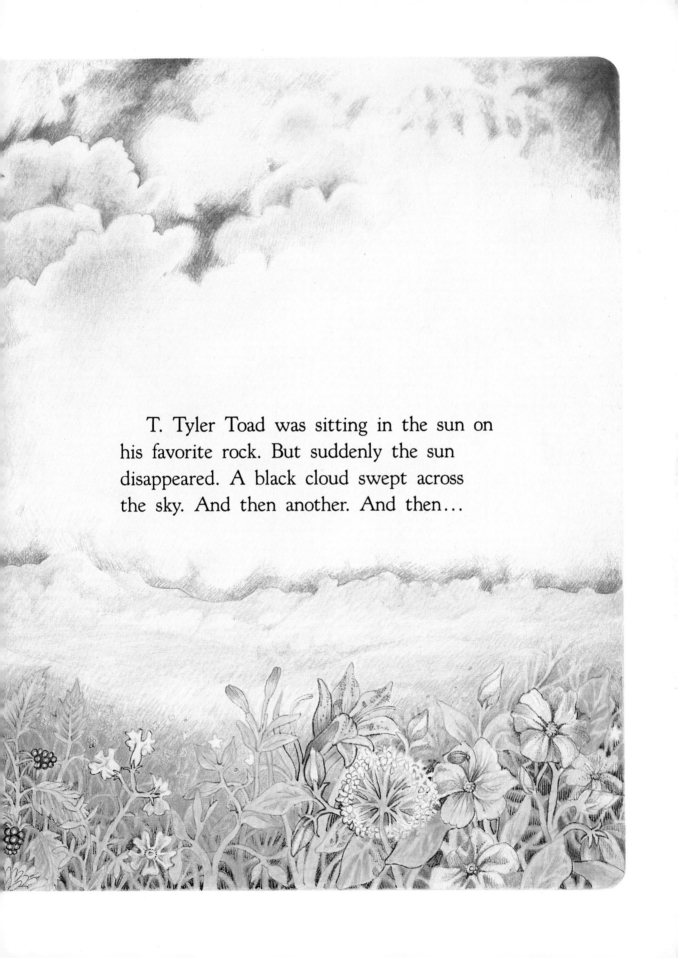

T. Tyler Toad was sitting in the sun on
his favorite rock. But suddenly the sun
disappeared. A black cloud swept across
the sky. And then another. And then...

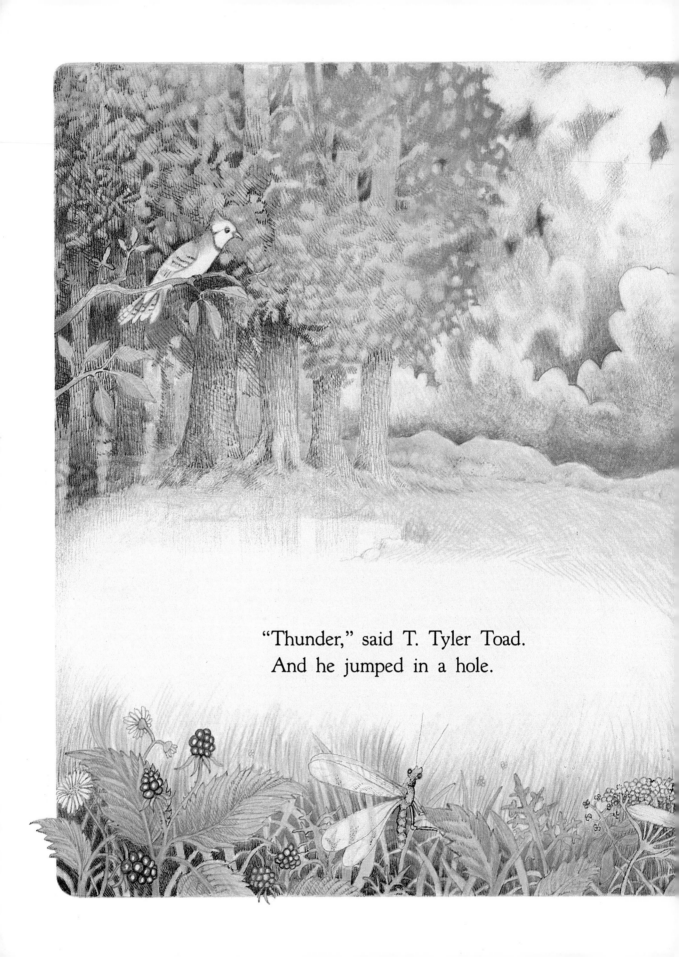

"Thunder," said T. Tyler Toad.
And he jumped in a hole.

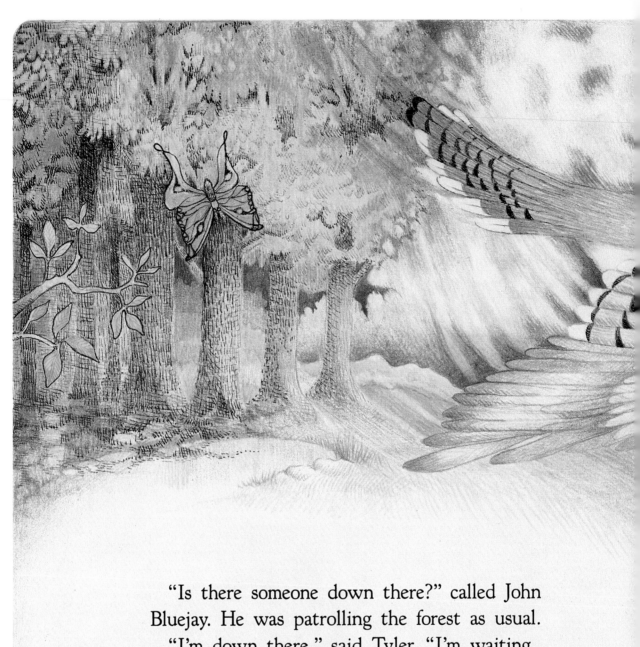

"Is there someone down there?" called John
Bluejay. He was patrolling the forest as usual.
"I'm down there," said Tyler. "I'm waiting
for the thunder to go away. It frightens me."

"Don't you know that thunder is just
the Milky Way Patrol testing their cannons?"
"That's what you say." Tyler shook his
head. "I'm not coming out until it goes away."

"What are you doing in that hole?" asked
Mrs. Raccoon, wiping her paws on her apron.
She had been washing carrots in a nearby puddle.
  "Waiting for the thunder to go away," said
Tyler. "I'm frightened."

"Don't you know that thunder is the sound
of the Sky Animals banging pots and pans?"
"That's what you say." Tyler slid further
back in the hole. "I'm not coming out."

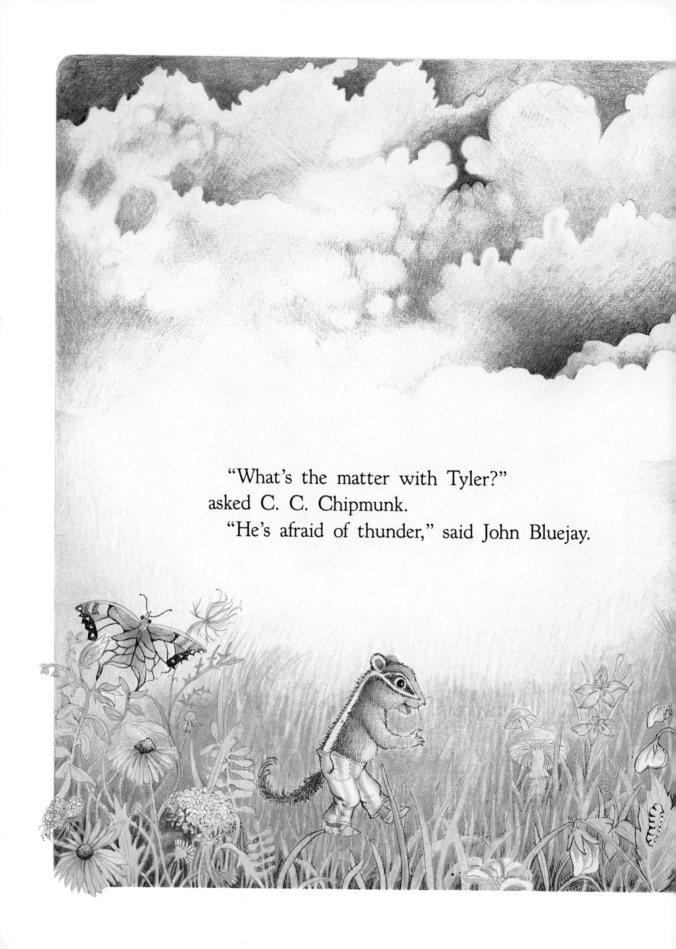

"What's the matter with Tyler?"
asked C. C. Chipmunk.

"He's afraid of thunder," said John Bluejay.

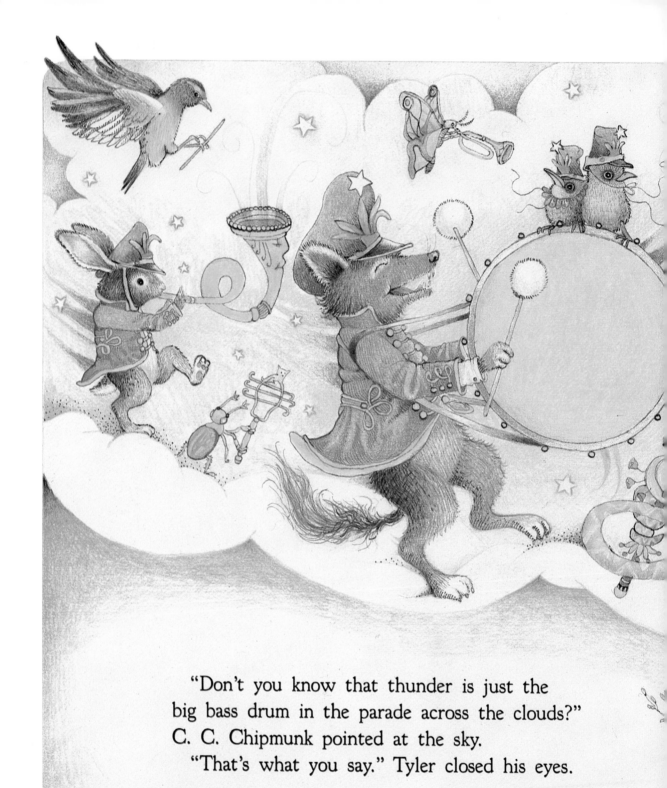

"Don't you know that thunder is just the
big bass drum in the parade across the clouds?"
C. C. Chipmunk pointed at the sky.
"That's what you say." Tyler closed his eyes.

Mr. Badger came waddling to the group.
"What's all the trouble?" he shouted. "Stand back.
Stand back. That frog needs air. Get him out
of that hole."

"I'm not a frog, and I'M NOT COMING OUT,"
said Tyler in a nasty voice.

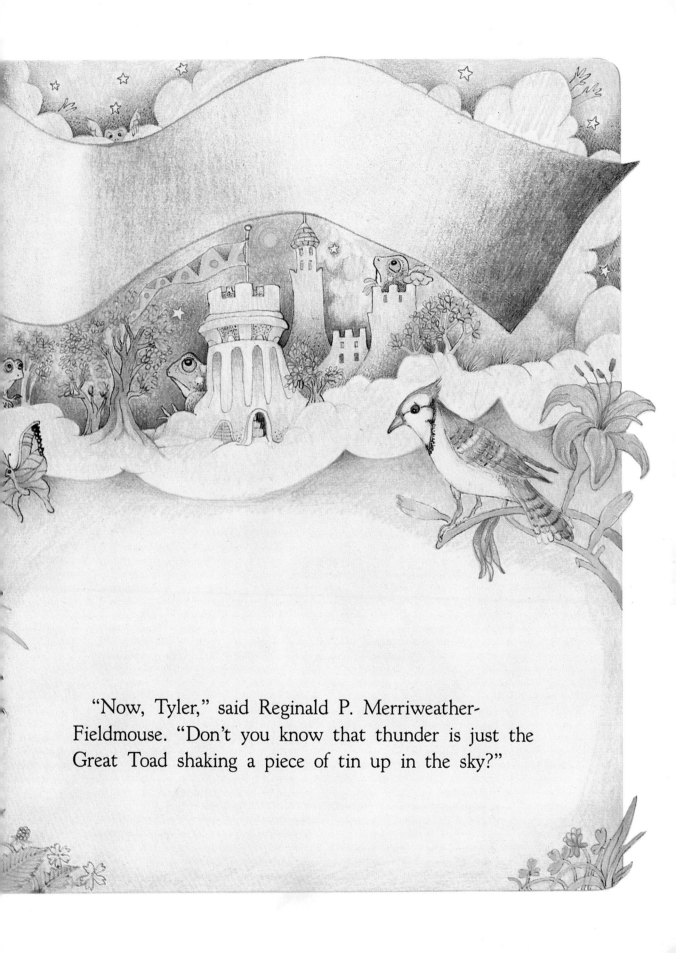

"Now, Tyler," said Reginald P. Merriweather-
Fieldmouse. "Don't you know that thunder is just the
Great Toad shaking a piece of tin up in the sky?"

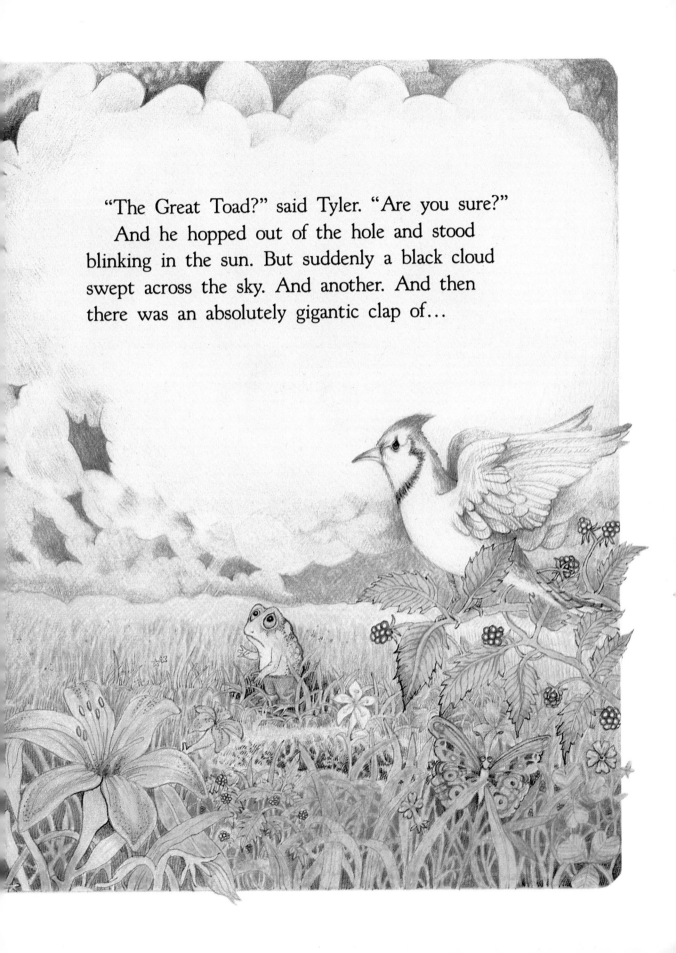

"The Great Toad?" said Tyler. "Are you sure?"
And he hopped out of the hole and stood blinking in the sun. But suddenly a black cloud swept across the sky. And another. And then there was an absolutely gigantic clap of...

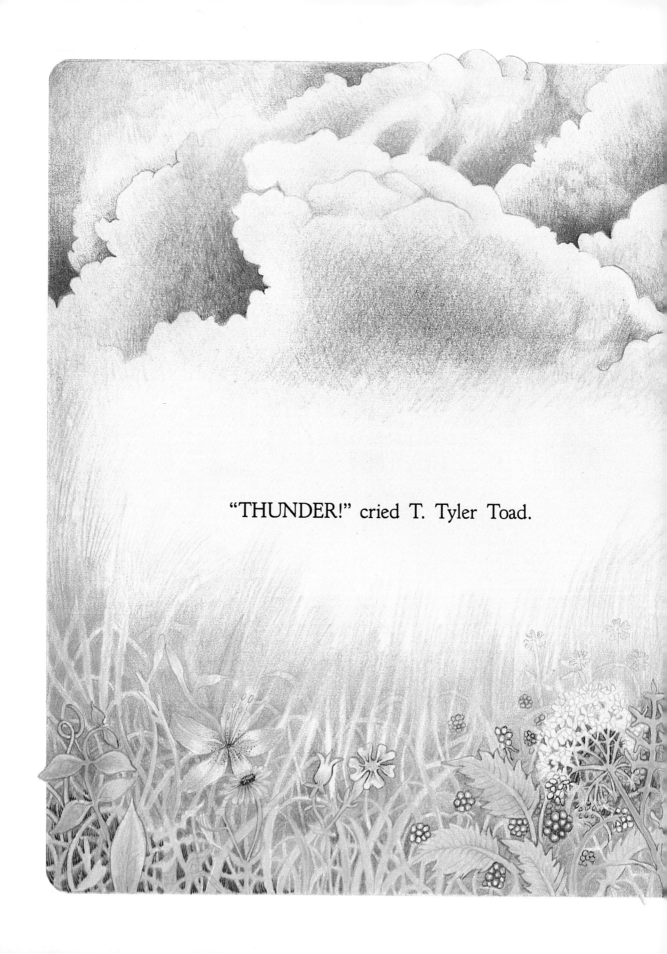

"THUNDER!" cried T. Tyler Toad.

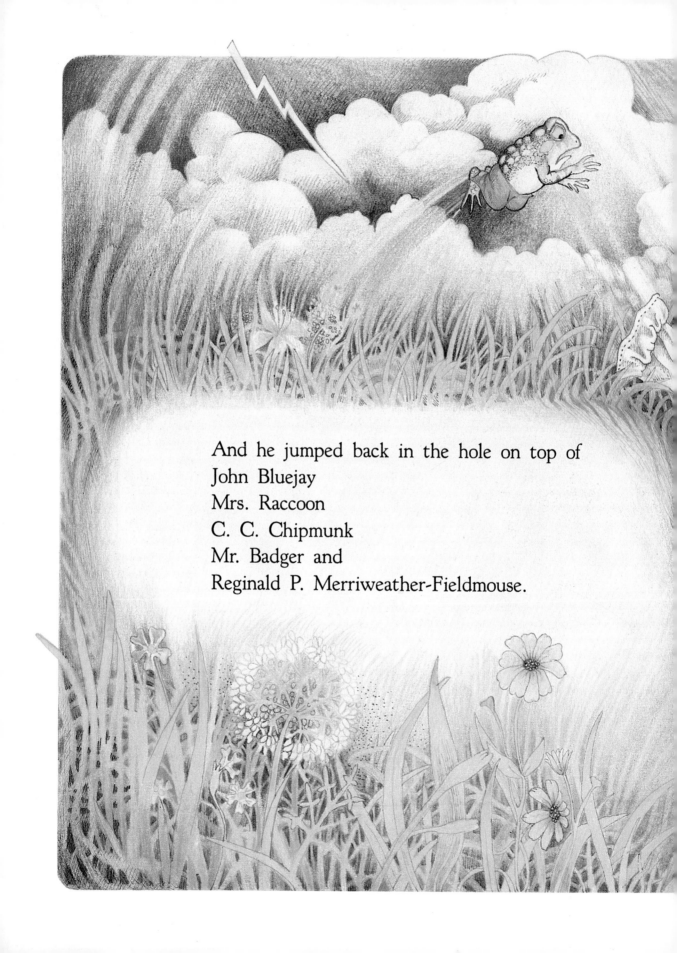

And he jumped back in the hole on top of
John Bluejay
Mrs. Raccoon
C. C. Chipmunk
Mr. Badger and
Reginald P. Merriweather-Fieldmouse.